VERTIGO

SCIENCE FICTION

BY ADELA ZAMUDIO

Translated from the Spanish by
LYNETTE YETTER

FUENTE
FOUNTAIN
BOOKS

Published by Fuente Fountain Books

1631 NE Broadway Street #737, Portland, Oregon 97232

www.fuentefountainbooks.com

Spanish-language Editor: Tania Cano

English-language Editor: Michael Favala Goldman

Author: Zamudio, Adela (1854-1928), Bolivia

Translator from the Spanish: Lynette Yetter

Title: *Vertigo: Science Fiction*

ISBN-10 0-9843756-9-4 (pbk : alk. paper)

ISBN-13 978-0-9843756-9-1

ebook ISBN 979-8-9912634-1-2

1. Literature -Women -Latin America -Bolivia -Science Fiction.

2. Title.

First edition, printed in the United States of America, 2025

Cover art by Lynette Yetter, based on altering a graphic purchased from VectorStock.com.

CONTENTS

INTRODUCTION

BY WILLIAM GILLARD, PHD

Adela Zamudio (1854-1928) is considered among Bolivia's most famous poets and was a force in the birth of feminism in that country and region. She was born to upper-class parents, but their favorable position in society did not last. When her wealthy grandfather died, her father lost his job, then lost his investments. She was taken from an elite private school and sent to a charity school for orphans and the impoverished. As was government policy then, girls were removed from school after third grade (Yetter 8). Her parents believed in their daughter, however, and continued an informal education for her, filling their house with books from Bolivia and beyond. She began publishing her poetry at the age of fifteen and released her first book in 1887. She was involved in the intellectual and art scene, wrote and directed plays, established literacy programs in Quechua for poor Indigenous people, edited a variety of publications, and continued publishing her essays, poetry and short fiction in newspapers, magazines, international anthologies, and in her final poetry collection in 1914, *Ráfagas*. In 1901, she opened an art school for young women. In 1920, the Bolivian government opened the first high school for girls, hired Zamudio to run it as principal, and later named it for Zamudio. She was the era's foremost trainer of teachers. Honors flowed to her as she was recognized as not just a great poet but an important public intellectual whose essays and art inspired change and growth all across Bolivia. Zamudio's birthday, October 11, is the "Day of the Bolivian Woman," a national holiday that celebrates Adela Zamudio and the contribution of all women to the culture and economy of the nation. During her lifetime, she was recognized internationally. Her first book was published in Argentina, her final book *Ráfagas* was published in Paris, and she was included in an anthology of Bolivian writers published in Paris.

Zamudio began her career publishing poetry: "her poems are the crowning jewel of Bolivian Romanticism and introduce some of the most significant literary innovations of the period" (Tenorio and Unzueta 366). At the start of the twentieth century, she turned more and more to fiction. Her best-known story is "La reunión de ayer" (circa 1915). Translated as "Yesterday's Meeting" by Lynette Yetter in her book, *Adela Zamudio: Selected Poetry and Prose*, the only English language collection of Zamudio's work to date, this story tells of a conclave of animals who come together to chart their future. They debate power and morality and interrogate their roles as predator and prey. This allegorical tale demonstrates that Zamudio's political consciousness was acute, since she apparently realized that it was more than education which would enable women to enjoy equality of privileges. Political reform would also be required. The male Tiger seeks the power that arises from its status as the most powerful animal (after the Lion, the King of Beasts), but the lying male Fox soon calls for the establishment of a new era, one based on rationality and reason. The conversation turns to humanity, whose technology allows them to move faster and fly higher than any other animal. The wise old female

Eagle asks, in all of this blind rush toward innovation and accomplishment, if humanity is any happier for it:

> Man has snatched secrets from heaven, from the sea, from the depths of the earth. Mechanics convert docile iron into instruments powerful, terrible, and delicate that grind, flatten, burnish and print [...] But a deaf and terrible thunder touches the lower layers of society; the foundations of buildings tremble. From poisonous caverns, wet basements, and workshops obscured by suffocating smoke, a multitude rushes out, livid, armed with explosive substances, insulting those above them by shouting at them: "You lie!" By placing the intellectual order above the moral order, you are wrong. Why would we want to be knowledgeable if we are not happy? (259-261)

In the end, the animals reject everything they know about humanity in all of its senseless and selfish cruelty. They resolve to live as they always have, confident that their way comports with morality and happiness.

"Vertigo" has never before been published in English translation. As an editor and writer of science fiction, I argue that, in this story, Zamudio used the tools of the emerging genre to her own ends, mixing them with elements intrinsic to Bolivian culture and not separated from her political activism. Unlike the frequent optimism of the science fiction produced at the centers of empires, Zamudio's science fiction bristles with skepticism about the nature of what others label "progress." Bolivian science fiction was undergoing a birth late in Zamudio's career, one driven as it was across Latin America by the arrival of transformative new technologies, scientific knowledge, and translations of seminal works by luminaries such as Jules Verne and H. G. Wells. By the turn of the century, Verne's books had swept across the world, appearing in translation in many languages and selling copiously. In the case of Wells, whose work saw Spanish translation as early as 1904 (Blanco 63), his writing became a small piece of the tapestry of *modernismo*, a movement initiated by Nicaraguan poet, Rubén Darío, and others in the late-nineteenth century that was influenced by European and Classical styles and emphasized emotional passion and highly stylized writing.

A focus on culture and nationality was also a part of the movement, both themes that rise in "Vertigo." Scholars are exploring the connections between *modernismo* and Zamudio (Ayllón 2025; Morales-Pino 125-148; Grau 122-148); it is perhaps likely that Zamudio was subject to the same forces that her contemporaries were and, as artists often do, engaged in indirect conversation with them. For example, Zamudio's short story "El capricho del canónigo" pokes fun at Rubén Darío's writing and what she considers the stylistic excesses of *modernismo* (Ayllón 2025). Furthermore, Zamudio participated in this literary debate as a critic of Daríos' *modernismo* because its aesthetics relegated the role of women to that of "muse" instead of being equals as poets (Echenique).

As Mexican poet Octavio Paz (1914-1998) wrote decades later about writers of Zamudio's era:

> [T]echnical progress across the *fin de siècle* world allowed for speedier movements between Spanish America and Europe. This "closeness" (cercanía), he writes, "hizo más viva y sensible nuestra lejanía histórica. Ir a París o a Londres no era visitar otro conti-nente sino saltar a otro siglo" (made our historical distance ever more palpable. Going to Paris or London did not mean visiting a different continent; it meant a leap into a different century). (Paz 6, translated to English in Blanco 59)

The give-and-take of style, content, theme, and vision among writers whose contemporary cultures were connecting for the first time using modern technologies is a key ingredient in Zamudio's literary stew.

Across Latin America, and in Bolivia in particular, the science fiction received from Europe and, soon, the United States, would undergo a blending with local traditions and tastes. Bolivia, in particular, already had a distinct language of fantasy literature that represented a blend of indigenous and mythological histories:

> Bolivian writers (and also foreigners) are drawn to thinking upon the nature of their mythical roots and their origins because of several factors: the fact that it is [...] the site of the ruins of one of the oldest cultures in the world, the Tiahuanaco culture; the proximity to the sacred Lake Titicaca; and the diverse geography that encompasses a good part of the Andes mountain range and portions of the Amazon jungle, as well as central valleys. The vestiges of Tiahuanaco culture, which preceded the Inca culture [...], means that thoughts of indigenous identity predominate in Bolivia, and with them mythical legends that have sometimes inspired texts, many of them fantastic. The archaic mythic component prevails in Bolivian literature of both fantasy and sf. (Rodrigo-Mendizábal)

Mixed into this focus on looking for creative inspiration is the idea that Zamudio lived through and actively participated in decades of radical transformation of Bolivian society.

Although the nation split with colonial power, Spain, in 1809, vestiges of the old colonial order still served as foundations for many institutions in Bolivian society: "Bolivia was built based on the patriarchal and racist structures of colonial society. This stratified structure of society aroused women's and Indigenous' rebellions..." (Allyón 3). During Zamudio's lifetime of activism, she "was able to establish herself as a well-known and respected literary persona and from this position, she advocated important social changes" (Barrero 95).

The movement for change in this area was so successful that in 1906, "the government proclaimed religious tolera-tion and permitted the establishment of non-Roman-Catholic churches" (Hudson and Hanratty 90). Despite the sporadic changes, the neo-colonial foundation remained difficult to move for most of Zamudio's lifetime: "Zamudio experienced the hypocrisy of living in a brand new country claiming to have thrown off the injustice of hereditary imperial rule in favor of a democratic govern-ment for the people by the people, but only for certain people that did not include her and all other women and all domestic workers, and all people who were not taught to read and write" (Yetter 7).

"Vertigo" mixes many elements so familiar to readers of Zamudio's writing. One reading of this story, for example, might see the story as postapocalyptic (for humanity). The passage of many generations gives the insects the neces-sary time to evolve a sophisticated knowledge of mammal anatomy (and tourism) that drives the story. The insects at the heart of the story might be the highly intelligent inheritors of an Earth that saw its last human long ago. Other readings are available, including readings that are not quite so science fictional. The depth and complexity of possible interpretations helps this story to stand as a great piece of Bolivian literature, an early example of global science fiction, and a landmark work by a Latin American woman.

Bill Gillard, PhD, is professor of English at the University of Wisconsin Oshkosh in the United States. He is a poet and fiction writer, and his most recent books include The Routledge Anthology of Global Science Fiction Origins *and* If the River Dies, *a young adult science fantasy novel.*

Works Cited

Allyón, Virginia. Prologue. *Adela Zamudio: Selected Poetry and Prose.* Translated by Lynette Yetter. Fuente Fountain, 2022.

—. "Re: Pregunta sobre Adela Zamudio y modernismo." Received by Lynette Yetter, 11 April 2025.

Blanco, María el Pilar. "Spanish American *Modernismo* and English Decadence: Beardsley, Pater, and Wells in the *Revista Moderna de México* (1903–1911)." *Modern Philology: Critical and Historical Studies in Literature, Medieval Through Contemporary*, vol. 121, no. 1, Aug. 2023, pp. 57–81.

Echenique, María Elva. "Adela Zamudio y la crítica literaria en Bolivia." *Retomando la palabra: las pioneras del XIX en diálogo con la crítica contemporánea*, Iberoamericana, 2012, pp. 305-319.

Grau Lleveria, Elena. "Entre el modernism y el patriarcado: *Íntimas* de Adela Zamudio." *Las olvidadas: mujer y modernismo: narradoras de entre siglos.* PPU (Promociones y Publicaciones Universitarias, S.A.) Barcelona, 2008.

Hudson, Rex A., and Dennis M. Hanratty. *Bolivia: A Country Study.* Federal Research Division, Library of Congress, 1989. https://www.loc.gov/resource/frdcstdy. boliviacountrysto0huds_0/?sp=5&st=image&r=-0.478,0.048,1.693,1.218,0

Messinger Cypess, Sandra. "Visual and Verbal Distances: The Woman Poet in a Patriarchal Culture." *Revista / Review Interamericana*, vol. 12, no. 1, 1983. pp. 150-157.

Morales-Pino, Luz Ainaí. "Más allá del naturalismo y las bellas enfermas: 'el velo de la purísima' (s/f), de adela zamudio y 'a caolha' (1903), de júlia lopes de almeida y la representación de la enfermedad como metáfora crítica de la modernidad industrial en el entre siglos latinoamericano". Literatura y Linguística N°45, 2022.

Ovando Barrero, Gabriela. "Three Women Articulating Their Voices from *El Chaupi*, in Upper Perú and Bolivia: Catalina e Erauso, Adela Zamudio, and Domitila Chungara." *Identity, Nation, Discourse: Latin American Women Writers and Artists*, edited by Claire Taylor, Cambridge Scholars Publishing, 2009, pp. 87-101.

Paz, Octavio. "El Caracol y La Sirena." *Revista de la Universidad de México*, no. 4, December 1964, pp. 6.

Rodrigo-Mendizábal, Iván. "Bolivia." *The Encyclopedia of Science Fiction*. https://sf-encyclopedia.com/entry/bolivia

Tenorio, María, and Fernando Unzueta. "Adela Zamudio." *DLB 283: Modern Spanish American Poets, First Series*, Gale, 2003, pp. 361-367.

Yetter, Lynette. "Domination and Justice in the Allegorical Story "La reunión de ayer" by Adela Zamudio (1854-1928), Bolivia." 2020. Reed College, MALS thesis.

Zamudio, Adela. *Adela Zamudio: Selected Poetry and Prose*. Translated by Lynette Yetter. Fuente Fountain, 2022.

VERTIGO

In a virgin meadow, where the grass formed a thick jungle from which slender carrot-family umbelliferae towered like palm trees, multitudes came to celebrate the arrival of the smiling Goddess: Spring.

It was the annual festival, always the same. The beautiful palingenesis of an ephemeral world reborn once again under the power of the season.

Seeds tore down their prison walls in impassioned uprisings. Larvae awoke. The hour had arrived for jubilant transformative journeys toward the light.

On that splendid morning, big and small, beautiful and grotesque, all in gala dress, mingled chaotically in a universal general strike. They floated with delight in the atmosphere saturated with moist warm exhalations.

All classes were represented in the diverse multitudes. There were toga-clad beetles, suddenly losing their seriousness, lifting their rigid elytra wing cases to unfurl the ruffs of their fragile inner wings. Orthoptera grasshoppers and earwigs opened their snakeskin-like fans. Luxurious lepidoptera butterflies of every kind: sometimes heavy and graceful like majas, sometimes light like grisettes; all painted with carmine or covered with gold dust. Here and there strutted bronze hymenoptera bees, ants and wasps, among whom buzzing horseflies took center stage. And everywhere gleeful throngs of mosquito urchins maliciously buzzed.

Scattered in the huge crowd, somewhat fearful of an unexpected blow from the police, low-level socialists also advanced: moths, grasshoppers and weevils, and their intrepid collaborators altica flea beetles and phylloxera aphids.

General murmurs arose when celebrities arrived. Noble inventors who provided industry with useful products, such as the esteemed chrysalis of an ancient silkworm reborn as a butterfly. A queen bee and her workers. A modest and altruistic cochineal. Or a friendly delegation of winged ants in their simple diplomatic attire.

Surrounding that brilliant constellation of esteemed individuals, anonymous masses swarmed. Myriads of nameless microbes, incubated in filth, turned toward the center of everyone's attention where they vehemently desired to be.

Below, in the shadowy avenues of the grass jungle, countless pedestrians ambled. Among the myriapods and arachnids was more than one sinister-looking character with the horrible gaze of eight grim eyes and a hidden poisoned point ready to stab and wound.

The festival was pastoral in the morning, but became a frenetic carnival as the afternoon wore on. Groups of imbibers toasted the Goddess as they worshipped Bacchus in the delicious chalices of flowers. The immense masquerade, deafened by its own universal grassy insect buzz, came and went in an endless procession around the meadow. In one area was a noisy and strident group of cicadas. In another, a grotesque group of pot-bellied horseflies, girdled in shiny blue and green iridescence, vibrated their gossamer wings like tambourines. Farther away, grasshoppers mingled with earwigs. And a merry troupe of butterflies wore long skirts whose garish colors contrasted with the aristocratic headdress of the short-winged and slender neuropteran ant lions.

Adjacent to this meadow ran a six-foot wide stream, which was a navigable river to these tiny beings. Many dipped their proboscises into its current to quench their thirst. Not far from the creek bed, sheltered by a stone hidden in the shade of a leafy pellitory, was a quiet spectator of the tumult—a bohemian artist cricket hiding his poorly dressed ungainly figure.

Evening was falling. Diligent luciola fireflies turned on their spotlights, signaling the party was nearing its end. A sudden breeze shook a rosebush arched over the water. Several petals fell. A pale dragonfly in the air folded its tulle wings and let itself fall exhausted into the hollow of a rose petal. The fragile boat, with its small load, rocked for a moment in a backwater and then floated away on the current.

The bohemian artist cricket let out a weak *cri-cri* and hopped from his hiding place into the thick jungle of grass where deep shadow reigned. From time to time, a timid moonbeam slid through the leaves and illuminated his steps. Alone he entered the deep woods that ringed the meadow. He wandered deeper and deeper into that night forest which inspired only gloomy thoughts. He saw no one. Everyone had gone to bed.

Suddenly he encountered the white dome of a strange building. It was a kind of rotunda rising above the grass. The architectural style was unknown to him. He approached, touched a wall partly obscured by an enveloping sea of greenery. Curious, he walked around the building until he discovered its entrance, brightly spotlighted by the moon. High up were two ovals or skylights situated equidistant from another. Centered between and a bit below them was an opening. It was a kind of mullioned window, whose central partition was half-ruined. A horseshoe-shaped portico guarded the entrance. But instead of columns, each on a base topped with an ornamental capital, the portico was adorned with a series of arabesques, like stalactites and stalagmites, carved in a harder and whiter material than the rest of the building.

The intrepid bohemian leapt into the building. Inside, an immense silence reigned. Frightful shadows invaded the corners. Moonlight streamed through the two skylights like the terrified gaze of a dying man. The moon's beams dimly illuminated the vault's interior.

There was an abrupt deep black hole in the floor of the vault. From the bottom of that cellar, the bohemian heard footsteps, and a voice asking, "Who's there?"

An ugly janitor, a beetle, slowly approached him. It had been a long time since the beetle had encountered anyone to talk with. The affable janitor welcomed the bohemian and invited him to tour the building.

"I suppose you want to walk through the ruins," the beetle said. "Follow me and think about what has happened in the past and today. This deserted vault, in whose concavity the echo of our steps resounds, once sheltered innumerable tiny rooms that were centers of prodigious activity. Within their delicate and flexible thin walls the highest manifestations of life took place. All of this fragile construction was housed here within this now cavernous vault. The construction was symmetrically divided into two lateral compartments, each of which was subdivided into three parts and surrounded by a succession of tiny rooms—all of it was contained within a closed gallery called cortical convolutions. The two wings of the building were connected by Varoli's Bridge (no doubt named after the architect who built it). These two wings formed what could be called the Central Office, since there resided the driving force of an admirable system of wires that connected the countless tiny rooms to the world beyond these walls. In that space you see there," the janitor beetle said, pointing to another area of the now empty vault. "A little below where the Central Office had been, were its subsidiary offices. They were responsible for activities on the ground floor of the building. The wires crossed at about the same height as the bridge, to connect the left and right sides of the Office."

The janitor continued, "If you look down into that dark hole through which I have just climbed you can see one or two steps. They are all that remain of the once grand staircase that led to the lower areas of the building. Each interlocking step had a hole in its rear portion. These aligned to form a channel. The bundles of conducting wires, which I mentioned earlier, threaded through this series of holes.

"Furthermore, the wire bundle was wrapped in a protective coating which prevented the special fluid the wires needed to be bathed in, from leaking out. That fluid then passed through the aqueduct of Sylvius to fulfill mysterious purposes deep within the Central Office."

The beetle waved his spiny foreleg in another general direction within the empty gloom of the midnight vault.

"Over there was Varoli's bridge, where pyramids rose on both sides."

The beetle paused to sigh.

"It is a pity that all these architectural wonders were carved out of such weak material that they couldn't stand the test of time. Today, all of the ephemeral Central Office with its many unusual features has long ago collapsed. All that remains, as you can see, is the solid part of the building."

The bohemian cricket listened attentively, even though the interesting and long explanations of his friendly tour guide, the janitor beetle, were starting to boggle his mind.

"Look at that irregular section of wall near the skylights," the beetle continued. "Because of its particular shape, it has been compared to a large bat. You can see that it consists of a central body and two wings that extend until they touch the two side walls. That admirable mezzanine joins the numerous pieces of the doorway to the vault.

"And beneath the bat-shape you can see a pile of rubble. It used to be a cribriform plate riddled with little holes. Air currents, hitting the interior walls of the lattice, covered with fine fabric, sent odoriferous atoms inwards, conducted by very fine threads that, passing through the innumerable holes, joined together inside the Central Office in two cords.

"This was the first of the many pairs of cords that connected the Central Office with various points outside. The active force that worked in them was not exactly the electric fluid, but something very similar. It worked in two ways: it transmitted the sensational news from the world beyond these walls into the Central Office, where it was duly noted, and then the fluid delivered commands from the Office out to the extremities of the building.

"Each of the openings in the doorway transmitted a different type of news, according to the region from which it came. These two concave skylights, now empty, were then covered with beautiful stained glass and curtains, through which penetrated luminous vibrations.

"Vibrations of another kind were transmitted by another pair of cords that started from two openings situated in the side walls, equidistant from the doorway. Follow me and I'll show you!"

They went out through the wide portico decorated with ivory stalactites and stalagmites and turned to the right. That side portion of the projecting wall of the vault formed, almost at the height of the skylights, a kind of roof, extending backwards.

"This roof," said the janitor beetle, "once bore the pompous name of Zygomatic Arch. There were two of them: one on each side of the doorway. I have two observatories on them. From here I amuse myself by watching sunsets or counting stars on clear nights."

They stopped at a point where the projecting part ended and the wall offered a kind of niche. Entering it, they went down an alley that led them to a small room where various objects lay piled up: an anvil, hammer, stirrup, and a lens.

"You will imagine that you are in a blacksmith's workshop," said the beetle, "but it's nothing of the sort; what this could be compared to more properly is a telephone office, although the apparatus you are going to see is more of a phonograph than a telephone.

"Look through that oval window, or this round one, and try to see inside. You will discover a horn that is tilted slightly downwards. That is the Eustachian tube.

"Have you ever put your ear to the shell of a snail? It is far from the sea, and yet you can hear the sound of the waves inside it. A similar phenomenon, apparently, although of a very different nature, occurs here. There is no life inside anymore, but the membranes that received and preserved the impression of the old sounds, although very damaged, continue to function—the air awakens them. The inner face of the vault acts as a vibrating plate that reproduces them and the illusion is complete. Try it yourself."

The bohemian cricket listened. At first he only perceived a dull noise accompanied by an ever louder resonance— then a distant beehive sound grew and became more complicated until it sounded like a great tumult. The more he listened, the better he understood. It was an entire external world reflected and echoed within, reproduced in a thousand simultaneous scenes, and at the same time, an entire internal life, subjective, hidden, that continued to vibrate intensely and painfully.

The dull resonance was becoming a prolonged aspiration, an endless longing, from whose depths arose the fluttering of palpitating wings that rose to infinity, the sound of waterfalls, echoes of the abyss, angelic cries, beastly panting, roars, death rattles, laughter, sobs...

The cricket suddenly felt overcome by malaise. He stepped back. His head wavered. And having barely time to say goodbye, he fled, stumbling madly. Then, with supreme effort, he launched himself in great leaps until he fell breathless, far from that sinister place.

The bohemian cricket's friends found him unconscious in the meadow's grass jungle and picked him up. His prolonged vertigo, from which they could barely rouse him, alarmed everyone. His friends, suspecting the cause of this catastrophe, told him about the pale dragonfly queen, the Grand Marshal of the procession, who had fled before their eyes the previous evening like an impossible dream. The mournful patient only smiled. He believed his illness was incurable. He became a misanthrope.

Lonely cantor of the ruins, the bohemian cricket whimpered feeble songs for the rest of his days. No longer the innocent soul of an insect, but a mad hypochondriac. Lost in depression. All because he had been initiated into the secrets of humans.

EL VÉRTIGO

A un prado, nunca hollado, en que la grama formaba selva espesa y sobre la cual se erguían, a modo de palmeras, esbeltas umbelíferas, había acudido la multitud a festejar la llegada de la risueña Diosa Primavera.

Era la fiesta anual, siempre la misma. La hermosa palingenesia de un mundo efímero que resurgía una vez más bajo el influjo de la estación.

Los gérmenes, rasgadas las paredes de su cárcel, se alzaban impacientes. Las larvas despertaban. Había llegado la hora del tránsito dichoso hacia la luz.

En aquella mañana esplendorosa, grandes y chicos, hermosos y grotescos, todos en traje de gala, mezclados, confundidos, en huelga universal, flotaban con delicia en el ambiente saturado de efluvios húmedos y tibios.

Todas las clases se hallaban representadas en la revuelta y heterogénea muchedumbre. Se veían allí coleópteros togados, que, perdiendo de pronto su gravedad, desembozaban sus hélitros rígidos y ahuecados, para estirar la gola encarrujada de sus frágiles alas interiores; saltarinas y tijeretas, ortópteras que abrían sus abanicos semejantes a serpentinas; lujosas lepidópteras de todo género: ya pesadas y airosas como majas, ya ligeras como grisetas; todas pintarrajeadas de carmín o cubiertas de polvo de oro.

Aquí y allí se pavoneaban los himenópteros bronceados, entre los cuales descollaba el tábano zumbón; y, en fin, en todas partes, la turba alegre de pilluelos, los mosquitos, igualmente malignos y zumbones. Diseminados en inmensa muchedumbre, avanzaban también, un poco temerosos de un golpe inesperado de la policía, los socialistas de baja estofa: polillas, saltamontes y gorgojos, y sus audaces colaboradoras: la altisa y la filoxera.

De repente, provocando un murmullo general, se presentaba alguna celebridad: alguna noble inventora, de esas que dotaron a la industria de productos útiles: una crisálida benemérita, antiguo gusano de seda, que acababa de darse a luz convertida en mariposa —una abeja reina y sus obreras— una modesta cochinilla, tipo de abnegación; o bien, una simpática legación de hormigas aladas en su sencillo traje diplomático.

Y en torno de esa pléyade brillante, la multitud anónima: miríadas de animaluchos sin nombre, incubados en la inmundicia, girando hacia los centros en que anhelaban ser...

Abajo, en las sombrías avenidas de la floresta de grama, se paseaba asimismo la multitud pedestre: miriápodos y arácnidos y entre ellos, más de un sujeto de siniestra catadura —torva la horrible mirada de ocho ojos y oculto el aguijón envenenado, dispuesto a herir.

La fiesta, pastoril en la mañana, se había convertido al declinar la tarde en carnaval frenético. Grupos de chupadoras aclamaban a la diosa rindiendo culto a Baco en el cáliz sabroso de las flores. La inmensa mascarada, ensordecida por su propio zumbido universal, iba y venía en corso inacabable alrededor del prado. Allá ruidosa y estridente estudiantina de cigarras —aquí grotesco grupo de panzudos moscardones ceñidos de luciente tornasol azul y verde, agitando sus alas de velillo a guisa de panderetas. Más lejos saltarines y tijeretas, o bien, comparsa alegre de mariposas luciendo luengas faldas cuyos colores chillones contrastaban con el tocado aristocrático de las neurópteras de breves alas y figura esbelta.

Junto a aquel prado corría un arroyo de dos metros de ancho, que para aquellos seres diminutos tenía el aspecto de un río navegable. Muchos sedientos hundían la trompa en su corriente. No lejos de la orilla, bajo una piedra sombreada por una obscura parietaria, bohemio artista, un grillo, tranquilo espectador de aquel tumulto, ocultaba su pobre traje y su figura desgarbada.

Caía la tarde. Luciolas diligentes encendían ya focos de luz. La fiesta iba a concluir. Un soplo de la brisa estremeció un rosal que inclinaba sus flores sobre las aguas. Cayeron varios pétalos. Una pálida libélula llegó volando a la orilla; plegó sus alas de tul y se dejó caer rendida en la concavidad de un pétalo de rosa. La frágil embarcación, con su pequeña carga, se balanceó un instante en un remanso y luego huyó arrastrada por la corriente.

El grillo exhaló un débil "cri-cri" y, a pequeños saltos, se internó en la selvática espesura de grama donde reinaba ya profunda sombra.

De vez en cuando, un tímido rayo de luna, deslizándose por el follaje, alumbraba sus pasos. El solitario se internó cada vez más en la floresta que, en aquella hora, sólo inspiraba pensamientos tétricos. No halló un transeúnte; todos se habían marchado a descansar.

Vagaba así, cuando de pronto vio destacarse encima de la selva la blanca bóveda de un extraño edificio, especie de rotonda, de estilo arquitectónico difícil de reconocer.

Siguió avanzando hasta tocar sus muros medio ocultos en aquel mar de verdor. Se había despertado su curiosidad y en un breve paseo de circunvalación no tardó en descubrir su portada vivamente iluminada por la luna. Consistía esta en dos óvalos o claraboyas situadas a cierta altura y equidistantes de otra abertura más baja, especie de ajimez, cuyo tabique central se hallaba medio derruido. El soportal que defendía la entrada del edificio era una galería saliente en forma de herradura, que en vez de capiteles, superior e inferior, ostentaba una serie de arabescos, a modo de estalactitas y estalagmitas, labradas en una materia más dura y blanca que el resto del edificio.

El intrépido paseante dio dos brincos hacia adentro. Reinaba un gran silencio. Sombras medrosas invadían los rincones. Los rayos de la luna, a través de las dos singulares claraboyas, adquirían la tristeza pavorosa de la mirada de un moribundo. Su reflejo en el interior de la bóveda difundía cierta vislumbre que permitía distinguir los objetos. En medio del pavimento se destacaba la negrura de una cavidad profunda como un pozo.

En el fondo de aquel subterráneo resonaron pasos y una voz preguntó:

—¿Quién va?

Era un escarabajo que avanzó lentamente.

El feo conserje, sometido a un largo ayuno de conversación, se mostró afabilísimo.

—Supongo que querrá usted pasear por las ruinas —dijo —. Sígame y medite lo que va de ayer a hoy. Esa bóveda desierta, en cuya concavidad resuena el eco de nuestros pasos, abrigó en otro tiempo multitud de celdas que fueron centros de prodigiosa actividad. Dentro de sus tabiques se produjeron las más elevadas manifestaciones de la vida. Era una construcción ligera, alojada inmediatamente debajo de la bóveda. Estaba simétricamente compartida en dos departamentos laterales y cada uno de estos, en tres divisiones rodeadas de una sucesión de celdas, en galería cerrada, llamadas de circunvolación. Ambas alas de la construcción, unidas por el puente de Varolio (llamado así, sin duda, por el arquitecto que lo construyó), constituían lo que podría apellidarse la Oficina Central, por hallarse en ellas el centro motor de un admirable sistema de hilos conductores que las ponían en comunicación con el exterior. En ese hueco que ve usted ahí, un poco más abajo de la Oficina Central, se hallaban sus dependencias.

En ellas se atendía al movimiento de la planta baja del edificio. Los hilos conductores se entrecruzaban a la altura del puente, poco más o menos, de modo que la planta baja izquierda comunicaba con el departamento derecho de la Oficina, y viceversa.

—Si usted quisiera asomarse a esa obscura escotilla —continuó—, por donde acabo de subir, podría ver uno o dos peldaños que aún existen de la gran escalera que conducía a los extremos inferiores del edificio. Cada peldaño estaba horadado en su porción posterior, de modo que, acopladas todas las cavidades, coincidían formando un canal en que estaba el haz de hilos conductores de los que he hablado.

En el pavimento de las divisiones de ambas mitades de la Oficina, se hallaba el acueducto de Silvio. Cerca del puente de Varolio se alzaban las pirámides: las anteriores y las posteriores. Lástima que todas esas maravillas arquitectónicas hubieran sido labradas en materia poco consistente. Hoy todo eso se ha derrumbado y sólo queda, como usted ve, la parte sólida del edificio.

La larga explicación del amable conserje había llegado a interesar al visitante, que le escuchaba con atención.

—Fíjese en ese pavimento —continuó—. Por su forma particular ha sido comparado a un gran murciélago. Mire usted, consta de un cuerpo central y dos alas que se extienden hasta tocar los dos muros laterales. Este admirable entresuelo sujeta las numerosas piezas de la portada uniéndolas a la bóveda.

Ese montón de escombros que ve usted ahí, en el fondo del ajimez, era una celosía acribillada de agujerillos: las corrientes de aire, al chocar con las paredes interiores del ajimez, tapizadas de fina tela, enviaban hacia adentro los átomos odoríferos, conducidos por hilos finísimos que, atravesando los innumerables agujeros, se unían adentro en dos cordones.

Era este el primer par de cordones de los muchos pares que comunicaban la Oficina Central con los diversos puntos del exterior. La fuerza activa que obraba en ellos no era precisamente el fluido eléctrico, pero sí algo muy parecido. Obraba de dos modos: transmitiendo las noticias sensacionales del exterior a la Oficina Central, donde se hacía conciencia de ellas, e impartiendo las órdenes de la Oficina a las extremidades del edificio.

Cada una de las aberturas de la portada transmitía un orden de noticias, diversas según la región de donde procedían. Por esas dos claraboyas cuyos cóncavos, hoy vacíos, se hallaban entonces revestidos de lindas vidrieras y cortinas, penetraban las llamadas vibraciones luminosas. Vibraciones de otro género eran transmitidas por otro par de cordones que partían de dos aberturas situadas en los muros laterales, equidistantes de la portada.

—Si usted quisiera molestarse, se las enseñaría.

Salieron por el ancho soportal adornado de estalactitas y estalagmitas de marfil, y torcieron hacia la derecha. Aquella porción lateral del muro sobresaliente de la bóveda formaba, casi a la altura de las claraboyas, una especie de azotea, prolongada hacia atrás.

—Esta azotea —dijo el escarabajo— llevó en otro tiempo el pomposo nombre de Arco Cigomático. Eran dos: una a cada lado de la portada. En ellas tengo dos observatorios. Desde aquí me entretengo en contemplar las puestas del sol o en contar las estrellas en las noches claras.

Se detuvieron en un punto en que la parte saliente terminaba y el muro ofrecía a la vista una especie de nicho. Penetrando en él recorrieron un callejón que los condujo a una reducida estancia donde yacían amontonados varios objetos: un yunque, un martillo, un estribo y un lente.

—Usted se figurará estar en un taller de herrería —dijo el escarabajo—, pues nada de eso; a lo que esto podría compararse con más propiedad es a una oficina telefónica, aunque el aparato que va usted a ver, más tiene de fonógrafo que de teléfono. Asómese a esa ventana oval, o a esta otra redonda, y procure ver hacia adentro. Descubre usted una bocina un poco inclinada hacia abajo. Esa es la Trompa de Eustaquio.

¿Ha aplicado usted alguna vez el oído a la concha de un caracol? Se halla lejos del mar y, no obstante, se escucha en su interior el rumor de las olas.

Un fenómeno semejante, en apariencia, aunque de muy distinta naturaleza, se produce aquí. No hay vida adentro ya, pero las membranas que recibieron y conservan la impresión de los antiguos sonidos, aunque muy estropeadas, siguen funcionando —el aire los despierta. La cara interior de la bóveda hace de lámina vibrante que los reproduce y la ilusión es completa. Haga usted la prueba.

El grillo aplicó el oído. En los primeros instantes sólo percibió un ruido sordo acompañado de una resonancia cada vez más fuerte —luego un lejano rumor de colmena que fue creciendo y complicándose hasta dar la idea confusa de un gran tumulto. A medida que se escuchaba, se comprendía mejor. Era aquel todo un mundo exterior reflejado y repercutido adentro, que se reproducía en mil escenas simultáneas, y al mismo tiempo, toda una vida interior, subjetiva, recóndita, que seguía vibrando intensa y dolorosamente.

La sorda resonancia fue convirtiéndose en prolongada aspiración, en un ansia inacabable, de cuyo fondo surgieron aleteos de alas palpitantes que se encumbraban al infinito, ruido de caídas, ecos de abismo, clamores de ángel, jadeos de bestia, rugidos, estertores, risas, sollozos...

El grillo se sintió acometido de un malestar repentino. Dio un paso atrás. Su cabeza vaciló y teniendo apenas tiempo para despedirse, huyó desatinado dando traspiés. Después, con un esfuerzo supremo, se lanzó a grandes saltos hasta caer sin aliento muy lejos del siniestro paraje.

Le recogieron sin conocimiento. Su prolongado vértigo, del que apenas pudieron despertarle, alarmó a todos. Sus amigos, sospechando la causa del accidente, le hablaban de la pálida libélula, reina del corso, que la tarde anterior había huido delante de sus ojos, como ensueño irrealizable. El triste enfermo callaba y sonreía. Sentía que su dolencia era incurable. Se hizo misántropo.

Solitario cantor de las ruinas, en su flébil gemido, desde entonces, solloza, no ya el alma inocente de un insecto, sino la hipocondría de un demente iniciado en los secretos humanos.

AFTERWORD BY THE TRANSLATOR
BY LYNETTE YETTER

Adela Zamudio created a literary puzzle when she wrote "El vértigo." She filled the story with scientific names and anatomical descriptions as mysteries for the reader to decipher. Since life today is so busy and few people have time or appetite to delve into unlocking the multitude of cryptic meanings in this story, I decided to make my English translation more accessible by providing definitions of the scientific terms, and by naming most (but not all) of the anatomical parts. I left some mysteries for readers to figure out themselves. I based my decisions on translator and scholar Michael Henry Heim's literary translation workshop model, on Quebec Feminist Translation Theory, and by my understanding and analysis of other works by Adela Zamudio.

I work in community by workshopping my English translation with other literary translators (most of whom translate from languages other than Spanish). This workshop model was started in 1964 at University of Iowa by Michael Henry Heim, with the premise that the English translation is its own creative work in English. Workshop participants critique each other's translations so that they read more smoothly and are engaging as English language texts. I consider all the feedback and choose how I want to incorporate, or not, each suggestion.

I also am inspired by Quebec Feminist Translation Theory which encourages the female translator to foreground women's lived experience and to exaggerate it in the translation so that it is more easily understood by readers who have not experienced living life as a female. In "Vertigo" the insects are almost all male, so I expand my interpretation of Quebec Feminist Translation Theory to strive to convey my intuitive, emotional and intellectual understanding of the story in its original language, Spanish. The "exaggerations" include defining the scientific terms, and naming anatomical parts, and also adding in a new sentence to help the reader visualize the setting. That new sentence is "The beetle waved his spiny foreleg in another general direction within the empty gloom of the midnight vault."

One anatomical term that both I and the Spanish editor, Tania Cano, labored over, was Zamudio's mention of "circunvalación." This word is often used as a street name for a road that circles around the outskirts of a city, intersecting with all the grid roads. But when looking at brain anatomy, the only circle I found was "Circle of Willis," a circle-shaped group of arteries that nourish the brain. But I wasn't sure if that was what Zamudio was alluding to as "a closed gallery" that surrounded and contained all the parts of the brain.

Inspired by Heim's workshop model, I pondered the conundrum with my colleague Tania Cano. She found that by changing just one letter, the word transformed into "circunvolación," the Spanish name for "cortical convolutions," the wrinkles of the brain. That made me recall that Zamudio biographer Taborga Villarroel in 1980 wrote that when Zamudio's family posthumously published her works around 1942, there were a number of typos and other errors. Because they were using whatever drafts they could find among Adela Zamudio's papers, and whatever other errors might have popped up through typesetting at the printers. Furthermore, the biographer said that the typos continued unchanged in future reprintings.

Aha! I decided that this must be one of those typos! So I corrected the spelling for the Spanish text that is published together here with my English translation. This is perhaps the first time "El vértigo" is published with "circunvolación," the Spanish scientific name for all the wrinkles of the brain (officially named "cortical convolutions" in English), instead of "circunvalación," the name of roads that ring cities in the Andes. Just changing an "a" to an "o" made all the difference.

Also, I base my translation choices on close readings of a variety of Adela Zamudio's other works. For example, Zamudio's circa 1914 allegorical story "La reunión de ayer" / "Yesterday's Meeting" is about animals gathering to debate the merits of progress and of behaving more like Man. I dove deep into "Yesterday's Meeting," writing my Master's thesis on my analysis of this story. So I felt compelled to spotlight the human aspects Zamudio gives the insects in "Vertigo." A bohemian cricket becomes a misanthrope. Insects are socialists afraid of the police. Mosquitos are malignant urchins.

It's notable that Adela Zamudio's writings over a hundred years ago foreshadow later books such as George Orwell's *Animal Farm* (1945). I wonder what other stories will be inspired by her writings. My hope is that these future authors will credit Adela Zamudio, and that you will enjoy exploring more of Adela Zamudio's work: her poetry, essays, novel, and her short stories including her contribution to the global origins of science fiction— "Vertigo."

ACKNOWLEDGMENTS

Thank you to everyone who had a hand in this book: Tania Cano for editing the Spanish language portions and helping untangle some of the puzzles in the Spanish text; the Tucson Translation Circle for close reading of, and astute feedback on, the English translation; Michael Favala Goldman for editing the English language portions of this book; science fiction scholar William Gillard, PhD, for writing the Introduction; Virginia Ayllón and Luz Ainaí Morales-Pino, PhD, Adela Zamudio scholars in Bolivia and Peru, for sharing your wisdom; the Fundación Culturál Torrico Zamudio in Cochabamba, Bolivia, for permission to translate writings of Adela Zamudio; and Fuente Fountain Books for publishing this first-ever English translation of Adela Zamudio's story "El vértigo."

ABOUT THE AUTHOR, ADELA ZAMUDIO (1854-1928), BOLIVIA

BY LYNETTE YETTER

Who is Adela Zamudio? This is the question I pondered as I faced her granite bust in the center of a small round plaza bearing her name a few blocks from where I lived for a number of years in La Paz, Bolivia. That curiosity drove me to read everything I could find by and about Adela Zamudio.

During her lifetime she was crowned with gold laurels by the President of Bolivia for her work as a thinker, and now her birthday, October 11, is a national holiday in Bolivia. Yet outside of her native country she is largely unknown.

Zamudio never married; she had no children. But she was a mother; she was the mother of feminism and women's education in Bolivia. Self-taught, she devoted her life to challenging the status quo through writing, pedagogy and teaching, literacy projects for illiterate Quechua-speaking mining families, and critical-thinking teacher training in order to change all of society for the better.

She was constantly learning. For example, when Maria Montessori's handbook about her revolutionary teaching methods was published in 1914, Zamudio was 60 years old and already the foremost trainer of teachers in Bolivia. Zamudio quickly embraced Montessori's work and started teaching her methods. I recently met with the grand-daughter of one of those Montessori teachers who was personally trained by Adela Zamudio. Aside from the keen intelligence of Adela Zamudio, the granddaughter remembers her grandmother saying that Adela Zamudio was brilliant; that she was very brusque in her manner, and butch in her presentation.

Zamudio's writings were mostly published in magazines and newspapers, which were the internet of her day, and just about as ephemeral. She was very famous, but like most women in male-supremacist societies, after she died her existence was ignored, marginalized, almost erased. It was only through the efforts of her family after her death, republishing her writings in a number of books in the early 1940s, that Zamudio's writings have endured.

In 1955 a biographer, Augusto Guzmán, wrote a short book about her life for school children. Feminist artist Judy Chicago included Adela Zamudio's name as part of her 1974-79 ceramic masterpiece honoring women in history, *The Dinner Party*, which is on permanent display at the Brooklyn Museum's Elizabeth A. Sackler Center for Feminist Art.

Then another biographer, Gabriela Taborga de Villarroel (Zamudio's grand niece) wrote a more expansive biography in 1980. That same year, a woman, Lidia Gueiler, was the President of Bolivia; she declared Zamudio's birthday to be a national holiday. Since then, second wave feminists and others have been writing about Adela Zamudio and her work, although mostly in Spanish. I am honored to be translating Zamudio's works into English, many for the first time.

ABOUT THE TRANSLATOR, LYNETTE YETTER

Lynette Yetter is a panpipe-playing Buddhist lesbian artist who shares her time between La Paz, Bolivia, and the unceded Indigenous territory temporarily called Portland, Oregon.

Pushcart Prize nominated poet, and 2023 PEN Award for Poetry in Translation finalist, Yetter first encountered Adela Zamudio as a granite bust in a park bearing her name in La Paz, Bolivia. Curious to learn more, since so few women are honored with monuments, Yetter read everything she could find by and about Adela Zamudio, culminating in a summa cum laude Reed College Master of Arts in Liberal Studies (MALS) thesis, and an ongoing series of books translating the writings of Adela Zamudio into English.

Other books she has authored include: *Lucy Plays Panpipes for Peace*, a novel; *72 Money Saving Tips for the 99%*; *El sincretismo de la Pachamama / Virgen María: la feminidad divina en Copacabana, Bolivia, siglo XVI*; and her translation *Adela Zamudio: Selected Poetry & Prose*.

Yetter's poetry, fiction, memoir and articles have been published in various journals including *Mantis*, *Foliate Oak*, *Sinister Wisdom*, *Western Tributaries*, and *Living Buddhism*. As a BMI composer she has recorded two CDs: *Lynette Yetter, Music of the Andes and More*, and *Espíritu Incaico/Inka Spirit*. Her award-winning music video, "Nam myoho renge kyo," shot to #1 as the most viewer-requested video on television in Oruro, Bolivia. She played panpipes on the opening title credits of the Academy Award nominated documentary *Recycled Life*. Her artwork has been exhibited internationally. Learn more about Lynette Yetter's music, movies, books, and art to touch your soul and make you think at www.LynetteYetter.com.

ABOUT FUENTE FOUNTAIN BOOKS

Fuente Fountain Books is an independent publisher based in Portland, Oregon, with distribution worldwide by Ingram. We specialize in progressive multicultural feminist books. We are a member of CLMP (Community of Literary Magazines & Presses), and a proud recipient of a 2025 Oregon Literary Fellowship.

Titles published and forthcoming:

- *Adela Zamudio: Selected Poetry & Prose* translated by Lynette Yetter (2022) (2023 PEN Award for Poetry in Translation finalist)
- *there are ginkgo leaves on the window: letters to my deceased grandmother* by Cara-Julie Kather (2024)
- *Vertigo: Science Fiction* by Adela Zamudio (2025)
- *Heaven Off The Coast*, a novel by M.S.A. Bacon (forthcoming 2026)

Fuente Fountain Books—where good ideas bubble up.

**FUENTE
FOUNTAIN
BOOKS**

www.FuenteFountainBooks.com